For
Jan Ann and Richard L. Kahler,
with love

www.randomhouse.com/kids

Library of Congress Cataloging-in-Publication Data
Phillips, Sally Kahler.
Nonsense! / by Sally Kahler Phillips. — 1st ed.
p. cm.
SUMMARY: Simple rhyming text and illustrations suggest that nonsense comes in many forms.
ISBN 0-375-83306-4 (trade) — ISBN 0-375-93306-9 (lib. bdg.)
[1. Self-esteem—Fiction. 2. Stories in rhyme.] I. Title.
PZ8.3.P558215No 2006
[E]—dc22
2004024089

MANUFACTURED IN MALAYSIA First Edition 10 9 8 7 6 5 4 3 2 1
RANDOM HOUSE and colophon are registered trademarks of Random House, Inc.

Nonsense!

Sally Kahler Phillips

Random House New York

What would you say
if dogs grew on trees,

if rhinos could fly,

and chickens laid cheese?

And what would you say
to a bat with a hat?
What would you say about that?

"Nonsense!" you'd say.

It's an excellent word
when you know something's really absurd.

What would you say
if mice lived on stars,

if rabbits read books,

and birds played guitars?

And what would you say
if a goldfish grew peas?
What would your answer be, please?

"Nonsense!" you'd say.

It's a good word to know
when you're sure something just isn't so.

What would you say
if pigs could sew quilts,

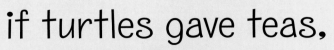

if turtles gave teas,

and fish walked on stilts?

And what would you say
to a camel in snow?
What would you say? Do you know?

"Nonsense!" you'd say.

It's the word to declare
when you know something's false or unfair!

And what will you say
if ever you're told
that you're not good enough
or you're dim or too bold,

or you're not very special,
you're strange or too shy?
What will you say in reply?

Will you sniffle and sigh
and assume that they're right?
Will you kick, will you cry,
and perhaps pick a fight?

Of course not! Instead,
you'll know just what to do
when you hear something truly untrue.

Only YOU can decide who you are!